On the Run

On the Run

CLARA BOURREAU

Translated from the French
by Y. Maudet

DELACORTE PRESS

Original French text copyright © 2009 by Editions Pocket Jeunesse, Department of Univers Poche.

Translation copyright © 2012 by Y. Maudet
Jacket art copyright © 2012 by Chris Sheban

Visit us on the Web! randomhouse.com/kids
Educators and librarians, for a variety of teaching tools, visit us at
RHTeachersLibrarians.com

Library of Congress Cataloging-in-Publication Data
Bourreau, Clara.
  [En cavale. English]
  On the run / Clara Bourreau ; translated from the French by Y. Maudet.
— 1st American ed.
      p.   cm.
  Originally published as En cavale. Paris, France : Éditions Pocket Jeunesse, c2009.
  Summary: Fourth-grader Anthony has always been told that his father is traveling, so when he finds out that he is in jail awaiting trial Anthony is upset and confused—but when his father escapes and takes Anthony with him life becomes really complicated.
  ISBN 978-0-385-74276-4 (hc) — ISBN 978-0-307-97706-9 (ebook) — ISBN 978-0-375-99076-2 (glb)
  1. Children of prisoners—Juvenile fiction.   2. Children of criminals—Juvenile fiction.   3. Escaped prisoners—Juvenile fiction.   4. Fathers and sons—Juvenile fiction.   [1. Fathers and sons—Fiction.   2. Fugitives from justice—Fiction.]   I. Maudet, Y.   II. Title.
  PZ7.B66833On 2012   843.92—dc23   2012010898

The text of this book is set in 13-point Baskerville MT.
Book design by Vikki Sheatsley
Printed in the United States of America
10 9 8 7 6 5 4 3 2 1
First American Edition

CONTENTS

· 1 ·

The Postcard

I got a postcard from my dad this morning. So did my sister, Lise. And my mom got a letter so long there were three stamps on the envelope.

There's a holographic image of birds on my postcard, so when you tilt it, it looks like the birds are flying. On the other side, my dad writes that his trip is going well. But I can't make out all the words because his handwriting looks like chicken scratch. The *U* looks like an *N*, the *M* like a *W*. It's hard to make sense of it all. So I ask Lise to help me. She won't let me read her card, though. It's always the same thing: she lets me look at the picture, but she refuses to tell me what Dad writes to her.

My dad travels for work, and he's been gone a long time. Two years, I think. I was in second grade when he left. He goes around the world, taking photographs of animals for magazines. We never see him anymore. I wish he'd come home. Two years is a long time to be without him.

I try to read Lise's postcard before we head to school. I sneak into her bedroom while she's brushing her teeth, but I've barely turned the card over when she comes in and smacks the top of my head with her hairbrush. She's smart, my sister. As soon as you touch her things, she has a way of appearing out of nowhere. Her mouth is full of toothpaste, but that doesn't stop her from shouting.

"Let go of my card, shrimp! It's personal. I don't go through your things, do I?"

My sister is always calling me shrimp. But one day I'll be taller than she is. Stronger too. Then she'll find out exactly how a shrimp takes revenge.

"But I let you read mine. It's not secret," I say. "You can look at it again. And I'm not a shrimp."

"I don't care about your card!" she says as she spins around and goes back to the bathroom.

On the way to school, I start telling my mom what Dad wrote to me this time, but she doesn't pay attention. I guess she's not interested, just like Lise. I'll talk to Hassan about it during recess. Hassan is my best friend. He has three sisters, so he knows firsthand that boys and girls don't act the same. Maybe he can explain to me why my mom and sister don't care about my postcard when I'd give anything to know what my dad told them.

Hassan lives in an apartment building at the end of my street. It always smells good at his place because his mother's a great cook. On Sundays, he and his father do jigsaw puzzles together. Hassan started one that had a thousand pieces, most of them just a lot of blue sky, which made it hard to finish. Sometimes I do puzzles with them and afterward Hassan and I play video games at my house. I'm way better at those than at puzzles because I play them a lot. Still, I wish I could do jigsaw puzzles with *my* dad.

We always have math first at school. This morning I hurry to finish the problems, then sneak a peek at my dad's postcard. It's really nice. Lise told me the birds were seagulls.

At recess, we head to the playground and I show my postcard to Hassan.

"You're lucky your dad travels," he says. "Mine never goes anywhere, just back to Tunisia. What does your sister's card look like?"

"It's ugly," I say. "There's a strange drawing in black-and-white. I like my birds a lot better. And it's in color."

Hassan nods. "You're right, it is nice," he says.

That's what I like about Hassan: we always agree on everything, except when it comes to Stephanie. She's a real pain. Plus she has ugly hair and her face is as pink as a pig's. But Hassan has a crush on her.

After lunch, the whole class goes to the track to run hurdles. I don't like the hurdles much, probably because I'm no good at them. Either I run too fast and knock them all down—and I get penalty points—or I manage to clear them but it takes me longer than any of the girls. It's a total drag.

To get out of running, I pretend to have a stomachache. I tell the teacher I ate too many baked beans at lunch, mine *and* Hassan's. The teacher asks if I want to go home. I hesitate. My mom's a nurse and she works during the day. I'd have to go to my grandfather and Yaya's (Yaya is my grandmother but we don't say grandma in my family, we say Yaya). I'd rather stay in school and look at my postcard. So my teacher puts me in a fifth-grade class for the afternoon, where the students have a history lesson on the French Revolution and how the people killed the king.

. . .

When my mom has to visit patients at night, Lise and I stay home alone. Well, not exactly alone . . . If it was just the two of us we'd pig out on gummy bears, huge slices of cake, and fruit juice, and we'd watch TV instead of doing our homework.

But whenever Mom works late, my grandparents come over. Grandpa and Yaya are my dad's parents. I don't know my mom's side of the family; they don't speak to my mother and I've never met them. At least, not that I can remember.

I keep saying that I'm old enough to walk home from school alone, but my mom won't let me. I don't know what she's afraid of. I don't mind so much when Grandpa comes to pick me up. He waits for me far away from the school door like I've told him to. But Yaya waits right in front, and she even talks to my teacher. Totally embarrassing! On top of that, Yaya dresses like an old lady, which I hate. The only good thing is that she usually buys me a huge raisin muffin on the way home, so I guess I can't complain too much.

During afternoon recess, my classmates are

still at the track, so I'm alone in the school yard. I sit on a bench and pretend I'm reading a book, but I'm just waiting for the end of the day.

Today, Grandpa picks me up.

I show him my postcard with the birds on it and he tells me that he got a letter from Dad this week too.

When I was in the fifth-grade class this afternoon, I had time to think about my sister's postcard. I decided that if I'm fast enough I'll have time to read it before she gets home from school. It's Wednesday, which means she'll be home soon, in about twenty-five minutes, so I have to hurry if I want to find where she's hidden it. I snoop through her things often enough and Lise knows it, so she constantly shifts things around.

When we get home, I don't bother grabbing a snack. I tell Grandpa I have homework and head upstairs. I go to Lise's bedroom and try to find her stash of mail. I have fifteen minutes left. It takes me a while but I find the postcard—right there, in the second drawer of her desk. There's also a pack of cigarettes and a lighter. I didn't know she smokes.

I'm careful to keep all the postcards in order as I start to read the first one. Something doesn't seem right: my dad doesn't talk about his latest trip. Not one word about it. Then I hear footsteps on the stairs. I have just enough time to stuff everything back in the drawer.

Then I dash to my room and pretend I'm reading. Yaya comes in without knocking (like always) to give me a kiss. She usually takes a yoga class on Wednesdays, so I didn't think she'd be over this early. She wants to know if I need help with my homework.

"No. I just have a math problem and a geography lesson," I tell her.

"You can go over your geography with me," Yaya says.

I sigh. I'm never left in peace for two minutes in this house. I'd like to watch my favorite cartoon, but now I have to do my geography lesson with Yaya. Great! There's no use arguing with her or I would. No TV for me today, I guess.

. . .

When Lise comes home, she and Yaya have a fight. My sister is fourteen years old and everyone says she's going through a rebellious phase. She swears a lot, which everybody thinks is normal. I'd like to be a teenager too, because when I happen to say a bad word my punishment is no after-school snack. And I love my afternoon snack.

I don't know what Lise and Yaya are arguing about, but they're shouting in the kitchen. Then I hear Lise stomp up to her room, and I hear her sniffling, like she's crying. I almost feel bad that I snooped around in her things.

I go out in the hallway and knock gently on her door.

She mumbles something and I open the door.

"Why are you crying?" I ask as I go in.

"No reason," she says with a shrug. "Everyone just gets on my nerves around here. We're a crazy family. We can't ever talk to each other like normal people."

"What do you mean?"

"That's exactly the problem. You're not—"

Suddenly Yaya barges in (without knocking, of course) and gives Lise a hard look. Lise starts to shout again.

"Is it too much for you to knock? I'm talking to Anthony!"

"Enough, Lise! That's no way to speak to your grandmother."

"It's better than lying to Anthony!"

Yaya yanks me out of the room and slams Lise's door behind her. Lise may be going through a phase, but it's the first time she's talked back to Yaya like that.

"What's wrong?" I ask. "What is Lise talking about?"

"Nothing, sweetie pie. You want to watch a cartoon?"

We head downstairs and I turn on the TV but I don't pay attention to the screen. I'm usually allowed to watch cartoons after I finish my homework, and sometimes on Sundays I watch sports with Grandpa. He loves explaining the rules of each game because he knows them all.

What made Yaya change her mind so fast? I

wonder. She leaves and goes to talk to Grandpa. They always speak in Catalan when they don't want me and Lise to understand their conversation. When I'm in high school maybe I'll be able to learn Catalan and understand all their secrets—and there sure seem to be a lot of secrets in my family.

For instance, at night, when Grandpa and Yaya come over for dinner and I'm in bed, I hear them and my mom and sister arguing. Lise usually clomps up the stairs to her room to let everyone know that she's hopping mad. Once I tried to go to her room and find out what was going on, but Mom heard me and came up to check that I was in bed.

Strange men also come to visit my mom sometimes. She always sends me out to the backyard before she speaks to them. I know they're not her friends: she only has girl friends, who bring us gifts or books. These men look at me and smile, but I don't like them. They smell like fish and never bring us any presents. In fact, they scare me a little; they aren't like other men I know. They're weird.

. . .

I can't fall asleep. In my head, I make a list of all the things that aren't normal in our family. At my grandparents' place there are pictures of my father everywhere. Here at home there are none. When I ask my mom why that is, she gives stupid answers like "Pictures gather dust and I don't have time to clean them" or "I have some but I keep them in an album. No need to show them to everybody."

There's something else. While I was waiting for my mom to come up and say goodnight tonight, I read my dad's postcard again. I wanted to compare this one to the others he sent me. I took out the special box where I keep all his letters. It's an old cookie tin Lise gave me after she decorated it with decals and photos of the two of us.

I never noticed it before, but each postcard has the same postmark—an image of a lake with windsurfers. It's strange. If you're traveling, the postmark should be different from place to place. Except, what if my dad is a nonmoving traveler? I fall asleep as soon as that thought occurs to me.

. . .

I wake up during the night from a nightmare.
I'm scared, so I call my mom, but Lise comes in.
She seems sleepy.

"What's the matter?"

"I had a bad dream. Where's Mom?"

"In bed. She just came home."

"What about Dad?" I ask. "Where is *he*?"

"Traveling."

"You're sure?"

"What's wrong, Anthony?"

"Nothing, I just had a nightmare."

"You want me to sleep with you?"

"Can we go to your room?"

"Okay. Bring your pillow."

I go to my sister's room and slide under
the covers. Lise crushes me with her legs but
it's not too bad. Her feet are ice cold, so I
put mine against hers to warm them up. We
call it playing hot water bottle. I never have
cold feet, so I'm always the hot water bottle. I
love doing this, except when Lise scratches me
with her nails.

Next day, I wake up in Lise's room. It takes me a second to remember what happened: the letter, the cigarettes in Lise's desk, the postmark with the lake and windsurfers, the nightmare . . .

I want to ask Mom about the postmarks, but she says she's running late and that we'll discuss it later. On my way to school, I decide to talk things over with Hassan. He collects stamps from Tunisia and maybe he knows about postmarks too. But we play during recess and I forget to ask him.

When I come home that afternoon, I go straight up to Lise's bedroom. There's something weird about these postmarks that I want to check out. I open the drawer and take out Lise's bundle of postcards. The cigarettes are no longer there. She probably took them to school, or maybe she changed the hiding place. I try hard to decipher the words my dad scribbled. Only when he writes to me does he try to write a little more neatly.

Not only are the letters mailed from the same

place as mine, but Dad doesn't mention his travels at all. He only talks about the last time he and Lise saw each other. And it wasn't too long ago.

I don't understand. Why has my dad seen Lise and not me? Why didn't she tell me?

At that moment I notice that Lise is standing in the doorway. She's probably been watching me for a few minutes. Normally, she'd have yelled and hit me. She takes boxing lessons, and I can tell she's making progress by the blows she gives me when we fight. I bite; she hits. It's about equal: I get bruises and she gets tooth marks. But now, she's silent as she watches me with Dad's letters in my hand. I feel my face get hot, the way it always does when I get caught doing something I shouldn't.

"I didn't want to search your stuff, I just wanted to check something," I tell her.

"So? Did you find what you wanted?"

"Dad doesn't mention his travels."

"No."

We stay quiet for a while; then Lise puts a CD on and we listen to the music, resting on her bed, not singing. I still have the postcards in my hands. She's the one who talks first.

"Is that all you have to say?" she asks me.

"Do you mean about the cigarettes?"

"No, who cares about that. I'm talking about Dad."

I nod. "The postmarks," I say, "they're all the same. Shouldn't they be different?"

She doesn't answer. I ask her again.

"Ask Mom," she tells me.

"She won't say. If you know, why don't *you* tell me?"

"I'm not allowed to tell you, shrimp. You're too young."

I bite the inside of her arm, where it hurts the most. I've had it with being called shrimp: my name is Anthony!

Lise cries out (she'll have a big mark tomorrow) and then she shouts, "Dad's not traveling. He's in jail! You know what that means?"

Yes, I know what it means. But it can't be true. My dad's not in jail, he's a wildlife photographer and he travels around the world. I bite Lise's arm again; then I run to my bedroom and lock myself in. Lise slams her door.

It can't be true. My dad's traveling, taking pictures of animals for magazines. Jail is for bad people. For thieves and murderers. My dad is no criminal. Or maybe it's like in the movies: sometimes good people are sent to jail, but it's all a mistake, the police got it wrong.

This is real life, though, not a movie. It can't be true. Lise is lying. Besides, my dad always initials his postcards *CR*—*C* for Cantes, his last name, *R* for Rafael, his first name—just like the letters next to his pictures in the magazines.

I head back to Lise's room, carrying a magazine.

"And what's this?" I yell as I barge in without knocking. "These are Dad's initials next to this photo, aren't they?"

"You're stupid! *CR* means 'copyright.' I asked Mom."

"What does 'copyright' mean? Explain it to me, then."

Lise sighs. "Ask Mom."

I try to do my homework while I wait for Mom to come home, but everything I read is a blur.

When I hear the car pull into the driveway, I rush downstairs. I turn the radio on, fill the teakettle, and open the door. Mom has barely taken off her jacket when I ask her where Dad is. She pauses the way she always does when we talk about Dad and his travels. I've never paid attention to that before.

"Why do you ask, Anthony? He's traveling, like always."

"Where is he now?"

"It depends. Why?"

"Because . . ."

I hesitate, and then the words fly out of my mouth.

"Because Lise told me that Dad's in jail."

Mom turns around and I see her eyes change and become very small and very dark.

"LISE!" she shouts.

My sister comes out of her room quietly. I'm

sure she knows what's going on, because usually when we call her she keeps us waiting at least fifteen minutes and we have to call her three more times before she "consents to show up," as my mother says. This time Lise appears immediately and looks at Mom from the top of the stairs.

"What did you tell your brother?" Mom asks her.

"The truth! Do you mind?"

"Yes."

"He has the right to know. Besides, he guessed almost by himself."

My mom starts to go up the stairs, and as she gets close to Lise I think she's going to slap my sister's face. Lise looks at her hard, sure of herself.

"Is it true, Mom?" I speak up. "I looked through Lise's desk and her postcards all have the same postmark, like mine, and Dad never mentions traveling."

Mom turns around and sits on the stairs. She smiles tightly. "His trips . . . ," she says with a faraway look.

Lise comes down a few stairs and sits next to

Mom. She's smiling too, not her usual defiant smile, but a serene smile.

A while later the three of us head to the kitchen and sit around the table. Mom gets up to make tea, takes off her shoes, and shuts off the radio. Lise helps herself to a cup of tea too (tea must be a girl thing, I guess), and Mom tells us Dad's story.

· 2 ·

The Story of the Cantes Men

"I met your father while I was working at a hospital in Toulouse," Mom begins. "He didn't tell me what he did for a living. I only knew that his father had been a burglar."

My eyes go wide. "What? You mean Grandpa?"

"Yes, and it soon became clear to me that your dad was working with him, that they were doing heists together."

"Heists? What does that mean?" I ask.

"It means holding up banks or places where there's money," Mom explains. "It scared me, but I tried to ignore it and act as if everything was normal. I continued working at the hospital. Your dad was very nice to me. He never talked about what he did. My parents disliked him, which is why we ended up on bad terms and why you don't know them. Eventually the day came when your father and I had to leave town in a hurry because the police had identified him on the security camera of the bank he had recently held up. I was pregnant with Lise. We went to Tangier, in Africa. Do you know where that is?"

I don't know and I don't care right now. I'll find it on my glow-in-the-dark globe later tonight.

I nod. "Go on."

"Soon the police were looking for him in Africa. They knew he was over there. They also knew that he had a wife and a daughter. So we moved even farther away. But Lise got sick and we came back to Europe to get her the proper treatment. The police were still looking for your father. We continued to hide. I started to work as a self-employed nurse; we made believe your dad wasn't living with us, and he disguised himself as a patient to visit us. I became pregnant again and the police were still watching us but we didn't know it. That's how your father got caught."

"How?" I ask.

"He came to the hospital when you were born."

"It's all my fault, then?"

Mom shakes her head. "Of course not, silly."

Still, if he hadn't come to the hospital, things would be different today. There's a lot I don't understand. My dad got caught, but I remember seeing him when I was younger. I have photographs and memories of nighttime train rides, the ocean, a fishing village. I remember that he taught me how to swim and that he carried me on his shoulders when I was tired of walking. I remember that he had a big beard.

Mom must have read my thoughts, because she goes on.

"Your father escaped before his case went to court. Nobody knows who helped him and he always refused to tell me. One night, while you were sleeping, he arrived with a car. We packed up and left."

"Where did we go?"

"To the seaside. Don't you remember?"

"I do. But I thought we were on vacation."

"That's one way to look at it. It was a vacation that lasted four years. We moved a lot, always to more and more remote villages, either by the sea or up in the mountains, or to very large towns. It wasn't fun, even for you."

For once, Lise agrees with Mom. She says that she wanted to go to school and have friends, but that Mom insisted on being the one to teach her to read and write. When Lise says that, I can see that Mom looks sad. Lise notices it too. I want to make Mom feel better.

"I'd love to be homeschooled," I say. "I wouldn't have to bother with grades, no report card to be signed—"

"Yes, well, it didn't take long for your father to see that living like that wasn't a good solution,"

Mom says. "You needed to attend school too, Anthony. So the three of us came back and he stayed away. You both went to school, and at last Lise had friends. We were watched; there was always a policeman in front of the house. They were waiting for your father. From time to time, friends of his would bring letters and leave them under the doormat. But it was hard for your father to stay away. He wanted to come back and see you grow up, even if it was dangerous for him. We called his lawyers and they entered a plea bargain: if he agreed to turn himself in, the court would take it into account."

"What does that mean?" I ask.

"It means he got a shorter sentence."

"And that was a long time ago?"

"Two years ago. Your father's been in jail for two years, waiting for his trial."

"When will that happen?"

"Soon."

"How soon?"

"Soon is soon."

. . .

I can't concentrate on my homework.

At dinner, I pepper Mom with questions. Is my father a mean man? Is she afraid of him? Why did he choose to rob banks? Why didn't he have a normal job? She tells me that we'll talk about it later, that I don't have to get upset about it. She also tells me that Dad never killed anyone and that I should never forget that.

She comes up when I'm in bed and shows me a photo of Dad with Lise and me on his knees.

She turns the night-light on when she leaves and I look at the picture for a long time. Later, Lise comes into my room.

At night she usually locks herself in her bedroom and writes in her diary, or she listens to music and dances. But here she is. She sits down on my bed.

"You're crushing my feet," I tell her.

She scoots over a little. "So what do you think? What are you feeling?"

"Nothing," I say.

"Come on. Dad's in jail and you're not upset?"

"I am upset. But it feels like a movie."

Lise sighs. "Well, it's not a movie, Anthony. It's real life. And take my advice: don't mention any of this to your friends."

For once she called me Anthony and not shrimp.

"Why?"

"You're so dumb," she says, shaking her head. "If you tell them, they won't play with you anymore."

"Why not?"

"If someone told you Hassan's father was a murderer, would you still want to play with him?"

"I don't know. But Dad's a thief, not a murderer. Mom said he never killed anyone."

"It's still the same. What he did is against the law."

"But it's only money. It's not that serious."

"What if everybody started doing what he did?"

I hadn't thought about it like that.

"Move over some more, I want to sleep."

She takes the pillow and pretends to smother me with it. Then she gives me a kiss.

"Good night, shrimp."

At recess the next day, I don't feel like playing, not even with Hassan. He thinks I'm mad at him and goes off with the other kids. Usually I don't like being alone, but today I couldn't care less. I imagine my dad robbing banks. Did he carry a gun? Did he wear a mask or a hood? It's dangerous to be a bank robber; he could've been killed. And maybe he did kill people. Mom said he didn't, but she's lied to me once and could be lying again.

Another friend asks me to play with him but I don't want to. I'm still thinking about Dad. If he has killed people, he could have killed Hassan's father or mother. . . .

In the cafeteria I sit at a table with some younger kids. Hassan saved me a seat next to him but I want to eat by myself. He comes over and asks if I'm upset because of Stephanie's birthday party. I'm the only one in the class she didn't invite. When I tell Hassan that I don't care about his ugly girlfriend's birthday, he doesn't believe me (or he doesn't like what I have to say), and he walks off.

After lunch, I keep to myself on the playground. I can't believe that my dad didn't kill anyone, ever. When they talk about bank robbers on the news, it's always because someone got killed. If Dad really did just steal some money, my grandparents or my mom would have told me. They wouldn't have kept quiet just about money. They lied to me again, I'm sure of it.

Grandpa comes to pick me up after school. On our way home, we talk. Mom told him that I know.

"Is it true that Dad never killed anyone?" I ask.

"Yes, it's true."

"Is it true that you held up banks too?"

"Yes, a very long time ago."

"Did you kill people?"

"Anthony, you have every reason to be upset, but—"

"Lise says that if everyone did what you did, everything would be a mess."

"She's right. It's more complicated than that, but she's right."

"So why did you tell me that you worked at the sawmill?"

"Because it's true. I worked at the sawmill afterward."

"Did you go to jail too?"

My grandfather takes a deep breath and starts to tell me his story. It turns out he was one of the most famous bank robbers of his time. Books have been written about him.

He worked alone for a long time, before teaching the business to my uncle and my dad. But my uncle didn't want to live like his father. He did well at school and went off to college. He never came back. He's a research scientist in Germany now. My dad wasn't like his brother. He thought robbing banks was a good profession. He decided to follow in my grandfather's footsteps.

Again I ask Grandpa if he ever killed anyone. He stops walking and lets out a deep breath.

"Yes, once, and it was an accident."

My grandfather is a murderer. Suddenly I feel dizzy. I feel my legs turn to jelly, like I'm about to pass out. I'm afraid to ask my next question.

"And Dad?" I say.

Grandpa hesitates before answering. "No."

"You're not sure?"

Grandpa looks at me. "Yes, I'm sure."

"Who was it that you killed?"

"I told you it was an accident. I'll explain it all to you when you're older."

"But I'm old enough now!"

"I promise I'll explain when you're older."

I don't pester him any more. I decide to ask Lise. She's older, so she must know.

When we arrive home, Yaya prepares our afternoon snack and Lise watches TV. Yaya wants to give me her own version of the story. I tell her I already know, but she insists. She repeats the things Grandpa just told me and says other things too. I notice that Lise lowers the volume on the TV and listens to what Yaya has to say. Since Grandpa is nearby, I don't dare ask Yaya why

Grandpa, who killed at least one person, isn't in jail. It's unfair.

For the first time, Yaya talks to me as if I'm a grown-up. She's very serious and her voice is deeper than usual.

Lise shuts off the TV and comes to sit with us. She wants to know why Yaya didn't stop our dad from becoming a bank robber, why my uncle went to college and my father didn't.

Yaya sighs. "That is the choice he made," she says.

"It was your duty to tell him that it was wrong," Lise argues. "Why didn't you?"

"Because it was his life, not mine."

"But you knew how dangerous it was!"

"I couldn't stop him."

"Liar! You're his mother. You should have stopped him! It's your fault he's in jail. You're the one who pushed him to do all this."

"Lise! Don't talk to me like that."

"I'll talk to you any way I want. It's your fault if we never see him."

Lise storms up to her room and locks her door. Yaya goes to the kitchen. I don't know what to do, so I go knock on Lise's door. She opens it. Her eyes are red and she's holding one of Dad's postcards. Since I have a hard time making out his handwriting, she reads them to me.

Mom doesn't come home too late this evening. I want to ask Grandpa how you hold up a bank, but it isn't the right time. Mom says she'll be visiting my dad in prison next week, in the visiting room.

"The visiting room?"

"It's the place where you can see the detainees."

"I want to go too."

"It's not pleasant, Anthony, it's grim. Not really a place for children."

Lise says she's not going. Sometimes it's difficult to understand my sister.

After dinner, when we head upstairs to bed, I hear the conversation between Mom and Yaya.

Yaya thinks Mom should listen to me, that it would cheer my dad up to see me. If anyone can convince my mom to let me see Dad, it's Yaya.

I go to Lise's room. She's cutting pictures out for her diary. I've already sneaked a look inside and I know she writes about her girlfriends and boyfriends, that she glues in pictures of singers she loves, that she writes about her dreams. It's a girl thing, totally stupid and useless.

"Why don't you want to go visit Dad?" I ask her.

"Because I want to be normal."

"What would that change?"

"Normal people don't go to jail. Now get out of here. I'm busy."

I brush my teeth and Mom comes up to say goodnight. I ask her again if I can visit Dad. She says, "We'll see." That means that I'll get to go. My mom explains that it will be a difficult experience, that the visit won't last long, and that jail is not a place for children. She explains that there are lots of hallways and metal bars and prison guards, and that I might not even recognize Dad because jail is a sad place where people change a lot.

She closes my bedroom door. I start to understand what Lise means. Normal kids don't go to jail to visit their fathers.

Lise is right. It is all Yaya's fault. She had no right to let my father do what he did.

I fall asleep, imagining jail like a life-size video game—gray, with metal bars and doors and endless hallways.

A few days before I go to visit my dad, the TV news announces his trial: "Rafael Cantes, the man who escaped police custody several times and finally surrendered, will go on trial soon," says one of the anchors.

At school, some kids want to know if I'm related to Rafael Cantes, the bank robber. I don't know what to tell them, so we fight. One of the kids tears my T-shirt, so I kick him where it hurts most—right in the groin.

· 3 ·

The Visiting Room

Now that I know I'm going to be visiting my dad, I count off the days in my math notebook. I use a coded system so if someone happens to see it they won't understand.

Only eight days left. Only four days. Seventy-eight hours. Just a few hours more . . .

Today is the day. Mom is picking me up at school, after the three o'clock recess. She wrote a note for the principal. I don't know if she said that my father is in jail or if she lied.

In class, I get the feeling that the teacher isn't

looking at me the same way she usually does. It's as if she knows. I don't want to attract attention or be punished, so for once I don't whisper with Hassan. He and I always talk about what we'll do at recess or when we go to his house after school.

I wait for the bell, feeling like it won't ever ring.

When I gaze out the window, I see my mom waiting for me in front of her car. She's early, for once.

At recess, Hassan asks me why I'm not staying. The teacher hears him. She tells him I have an appointment and it's none of his business. It must mean she knows where I'm going. She's nicer than I thought.

In the car, I want to talk to Mom, to ask her questions about the jail, but I can see that it's not the right time: she's tense, impatient at red lights, grumbling about the pedestrians and all the people who don't know how to drive.

I try to imagine what a real jail will be like. In comic books, everything is gray, rooms are like high-walled cubes, criminals are in drab pajamas, and the guards keep an eye on them with big rifles. In movies, it's less gloomy but more frightening.

Mom turns off the radio, which means we must be getting close. Traffic circles, large empty spaces, a dump, some fields, one more traffic circle. I look at the road signs, but I don't see any for a jail anywhere. We finally make a turn at a sign that has DETENTION CENTER written on it.

The jail doesn't look like my idea of a jail but like a hospital. It's white and seems very clean, and there are lots of guards, just watching. We park in an area for visitors. My mom checks her makeup, combs her hair, and puts some perfume on (too much, it stinks). She combs my hair, even though she knows I don't like that. I don't complain and let her flatten it. I asked Lise to shape my hair with gel this morning.

We wait in front of an entrance where a line has already formed. Mom constantly checks to make sure she has her ID. Afterward, everything is a blur of white hallways and metal bars. But I'll always remember the smell. It's even worse than bleach. It smells clean and dirty all at once. My stomach gets upset: I feel like puking. Mom takes hold of my hand and I follow her.

We're searched a few times and everyone has to leave their keys, purses, and cell phones in a bin. I don't whine.

We finally reach the visiting room. It's furnished with round tables where men are sitting and looking at the door. When we walk in, a man gets up. There are two guards near him. Mom smiles at the man. I think I recognize him. It's my dad.

At some tables around us, I see other children, some of them very young, even some babies.

I feel intimidated. I thought we'd be alone. Mom told me that on visiting days whole families are allowed to come, but I didn't think we'd all be in the same room. I see a girl about my age. She takes a large envelope and slides out a few drawings and a notebook. She hands the drawings to a man I guess is her father. At first I think she's showing him her homework, but it can't be homework, because he keeps everything.

While Mom talks to Dad, I look at the other prisoners. There are young ones and old ones, but more young than old. Their girlfriends and wives are crying or kissing them. I didn't notice whether my mom kissed my dad.

I'm afraid to go too close to my dad. He probably notices. I wonder if he blames me for his getting caught after I was born. He doesn't mention it. He just tells me that he's happy to see me. That it was time for me to know the truth. I'm old enough now.

He takes a good long look at me. He doesn't look the way I remember him. I remember him as very tanned, with a large beard that tickles. Now he's not tanned, his skin looks a little yellow (but maybe that's because of the neon light: everybody seems yellow), and his beard and whiskers are gone. I liked his bristly beard.

Before we came I asked Mom if I'm allowed to take pictures but she said no. Mom doesn't like pictures. "Don't worry, you'll remember what he looks like after you visit," she told me. "Pictures are for people who have no memory."

Dad asks me if I'm happy to see him, if I was scared to come to a prison. I tell him that it reminds me of a hospital and that it smells bad. I tell him that I'm sorry he's in jail because of me. He doesn't understand. So I explain that Mom told me he was caught when he visited me in the hospital after I was born. That makes him laugh.

"I would have given myself up sooner or later," he says.

I keep looking at him to make sure I'll remember him. I don't speak much after that because I don't want people to overhear me. I'm afraid to ask questions. I guess I really don't know my dad anymore.

Mom is the one who talks now. Eventually she tells Dad that Lise got into another fight at school. Without thinking, I blurt out that Lise is teaching me boxing moves, like how to bob and weave . . . in case someone bothers me.

"Why? Are you being bullied?"

"No. Just in case. Lise is strong. She won all her fights at the club last month."

My father smiles, which makes me happy.

Then I just listen to my parents talk. They discuss the upcoming trial, the testimony my mom and my grandparents will give. My dad says that my other grandparents (my mother's parents) will also be there, the grandparents I don't know. He and my mom talk about friends of my dad's who'll attend the trial, about the witnesses the lawyers will call. They mention journalists who'll be covering the trial, and my dad says that we'll have to be very careful who we talk to. He says the same thing to me as Mom and Yaya: "If a stranger talks to you in the street, don't answer him, don't follow him, don't show him your notebooks or your toys, even if he promises to give you a video game."

Around us, kids are laughing and talking to their fathers like it's totally normal to be here.

· · ·

On the way home, I notice that Mom is crying. I turn on the radio. We sing and her tears dry up. Then we go food shopping, a special shopping trip to celebrate. Lise is waiting for us when we get back and we make crepes.

I start a special notebook that I call "The Visiting Room." I'm going to write down what Dad says to me, just like Lise writes things in her diary. Except I'm not going to put pictures of any singers in there. Lise comes in before I have time to hide my secret notebook.

"So?" she says. "How did it go?"

"Why didn't you come if you want to know?"

She doesn't like my answer and grabs me from behind. I fall off my chair.

It hurts but I'm not about to cry.

"Did that hurt?"

"No."

"Liar. So, does it stink enough in jail?"

"How do you know?"

"I went there before you."

"And why don't you want to go anymore?"

"There's no point. And like I already told you, I want to be normal."

"Mom told him about your boxing."

"Really?"

"Yeah."

"Did you tell him I won?"

I nod. "Yeah."

She finally lets go of me. "Good, shrimp," she says. "Have a good night."

In school the next day, Hassan asks me why I had to leave early the day before. I decide to tell him the truth because he's my friend and has a right to know.

"I went to see my dad."

"He's not traveling?"

I hesitate. "Not really. Not right now, at least."

Hassan makes believe he understands, just like I make believe I'm telling the truth.

"Okay. Cool. Did he bring you any presents?"

Suddenly I chicken out. I understand what

Lise was trying to tell me. If I ever blurt out that my dad's in jail, even Hassan, my best friend, might call me a liar and turn on me. He might even tell ugly Stephanie, and she would blab it to everybody.

I play by myself during both recess periods; I don't want Hassan to ask me any more questions. Actually, he couldn't care less: he's kissing Stephanie—in front of everyone. Really, I don't get what he sees in her.

During the afternoon recess, Bruno comes to see if I'll play with him. Usually Bruno is all alone during recess; he has no friends. We make fun of him because he's two years older than the rest of us in class. He probably noticed that I was alone. He asks me why I'm not playing with the others. I tell him it's none of his business, and tears flood his eyes (a real baby). I would have laughed at him before, but not this time. I start to tell him about my dad, but I don't know if he believes me; I can see him knit his eyebrows. We go back to class. I'm afraid Bruno will repeat what I just told him, but since he has no friends, he has no one to talk to.

Now I go to the visiting room every Wednesday. I recognize the other kids who come to see their fathers. I talk to a girl who's as old as Lise. She can't come every week because she lives too far away: it's a four-hour drive. So she's here every other week, with her older sister and her mother. She says I'm lucky to live close to the detention center.

I make drawings and think of questions for my dad; I tell him what I did during the week, if I had a fight with Lise, if we've been punished, if I won my soccer match or not. I tell him what we do on weekends. Lise still refuses to visit. She always has a good excuse: too much work, a boxing lesson, a dance rehearsal at one of her friends'. But none of us are dumb; we all know she just doesn't want to come.

But one night, as I'm doing my homework, Lise enters my bedroom without knocking and hands me an envelope. She knows Mom and I are going to the visiting room the next day.

"Here, shrimp," she says. "Give this to Dad."

I'm about to ask her why she won't go herself but, for once, I don't. I see that she's taped the back of the envelope.

"Don't even try to open it or I'll break both your arms," Lise says.

I put her envelope inside my visiting room notebook.

The following day, when I give her letter to Dad, he seems happier than when I bring my drawings. It makes me jealous and glad at the same time.

We learn that Dad's trial is set to begin in a few days. It's mentioned on the evening news, before anything else, before the Israel-Palestine conflict, before the space walk, before the local strikes, before the flood reports. My dad's story is at the top of the news hour!

I'm getting dinner ready with Mom while Lise gabs on the phone. Mom wants to know what I did at school; she tells me what she did at work; we listen to the radio; we wait for Lise (who's blabbing away) and for the pasta water to boil. Mom puts some tomatoes in the oven.

As we wait for everything to cook, Mom turns on the TV. We watch a game show; then the news starts. And my dad comes on the screen.

I don't recognize him right away. The newsman shows a black-and-white photo of Dad that I've never seen before.

It's a scary photo, with Dad looking straight ahead, bug-eyed. It's an ugly picture, and there's a stain on it.

That's when the tomatoes start to burn. Mom doesn't notice because she's looking at the TV. The newscaster explains that the Cantes trial is about to begin. I think it's rude not to give my dad's full name, Rafael Cantes.

They show other photos of my dad, of the banks he robbed, and they interview some of the bank employees. "It happened so quickly," one says. "He was armed but he didn't use his weapon."

"We were scared," says another, "but he left the same way he came in."

The newsman says that Cantes was working alone, that he had already been arrested once, that he had gone into hiding in Africa years before. They question his lawyer, a fat man with his hair in a ponytail. I remember seeing him at our house. He's the one who smells like fish. He's a good speaker who says that my dad never used his gun. That he never killed anyone.

We don't watch the end of the news. Mom opens the oven; the tomatoes are like charcoal. We eat the pasta without them.

Lise wants to know if Mom is going to attend the trial and if we'll have to as well. Mom just says that we should continue to live our lives as usual but that we have to be extra careful in the street.

"Why?"

"Because journalists will probably try to take

pictures of you. I already talked to the principals at your schools, but you never know."

I don't see why journalists would be interested in Lise and me.

The next day I begin to understand.

All my classmates heard the news. Some brought their parents' newspapers to school, even though they never read anything, not even comic books. Maybe the teacher will give them extra credit for it.

In the school yard they all come over to me, especially older kids from the sixth grade.

I'm surrounded. Everyone is looking at me, when yesterday most of them didn't know who I was.

"So? Your dad? Did he kill people?" one kid asks.

"No! He just robbed banks. He's not a murderer."

Bruno is one of the kids who says nasty things. I guess he's happy to be on the side of the strong ones for a change. But I'm not a baby and I don't cry.

Hassan comes to my rescue—until Stephanie starts to meddle.

"Yeah! In any case," she says, "my mother doesn't want me to talk to you."

"I'm not surprised, if she's as stupid as you," I shoot back. "Anyway, I don't want to talk to you either."

She's about to cry but Hassan takes her side.

"You can't say bad things about other people's parents," he says to me. "It's not cool."

"Wait a minute! Didn't you hear what she said about my dad?"

Stephanie takes Hassan's arm. "Come on, Hassan! You can't hang around him anymore."

Hassan hesitates but leaves with her. Later, in the cafeteria, Hassan winks at me as if to tell me he's sorry, that we're still friends, but I eat alone anyway.

I can't wait for the end of the school day so I can go home.

. . .

Now I understand why Lise wants to be normal.

She's probably going through the same thing at her school, because tonight Lise doesn't call any of her friends and she's all moody, slamming doors and playing loud music in her room.

As we're setting the table for dinner, a man rings our bell: he wants to take some pictures. Mom gets really angry. She tells him off with words I've never heard before. She pushes him outside and threatens to call the police. He still manages to take a picture as Mom gives him a last shove. She's very upset.

I want to tell her what happened at school but I don't. We eat in silence and we watch the news.

While we're brushing our teeth, Lise tells me that Mom is going to testify tomorrow. That's why Mom is on edge. Lise explains to me what happens during a trial; she looked it up on the Internet at school (because at home, the computer is in Mom's room and she'd know it if we used it without telling her). I tell Lise about all the kids who came up to me at recess, even the older ones, and how Bruno sided with the others. She looks at me and says that if I keep getting bothered, she'll personally take care of it. In the meantime, she teaches me new ways to defend myself.

"You don't look at them, they don't look at you," she tells me. "You don't speak to them, they don't speak to you. And if they pick a fight with you, do what I just showed you."

My dad has been on the TV news for the last three days. I've had it!

I don't want to go to school anymore. I have no friends now; only the older kids want to talk to me, and it's always to ask questions about my dad. In class, I have the feeling everyone is making fun of me.

Even my teacher is acting differently. If I misbehave, she scolds me more than she does the others, but when someone picks on me, she always comes to my defense. Still, with the new boxing moves Lise taught me, I can take care of myself, without her help.

• 4 •

The Escape

On TV, they announce Dad's escape. Some-how he managed to get away just as he was about to leave the courthouse to go back to jail. That's the big scoop of the day for the news-people. Some witnesses tell the journalists that it happened very fast and that he probably had help. He was in a room guarded by policemen when he fainted. They opened the window while they waited for the ambulance to arrive; Dad ran to the window and slid down along a gutter. He mounted a scooter that was waiting for him in the street. Then he vanished, without a trace.

. . .

The phone rings right after the news. It's Grandpa. He wants to speak to my mom. I hear him say, "It can't be true, it can't be true." Mom isn't trying to hide her tears. Lise is the one who makes dinner—half-cooked rice with rubbery chicken (she's lousy at cooking; the only thing she doesn't mess up is yogurt cake). Mom tells us she has to visit a patient tonight. It's a lie: there's no appointment on her calendar. Does she really think we're that dumb? We know she's going to my grandparents' to talk about Dad. Why can't we just talk to one another like a normal family?

Usually when we're alone, Lise and I like to watch TV, but tonight we clean up the kitchen. Lise washes the dishes and I dry. We put our pajamas on and we stay in Lise's room, where we play cards without fighting, and we don't mention Dad's escape. But we don't think about anything else. We know it's serious. I want to ask Lise a few questions but I can see that she wants to cry too.

It's late when Mom gets back, but I'm not

sleeping. My glow-in-the-dark globe lights up my room. She comes over to kiss me before going to speak to Lise for a long time. I want to listen to what they're saying, but I fall asleep.

The next morning when we go out, I see a car stationed in front of the house. Inside the car, there's a man reading a newspaper. My mom goes over to talk to him.

"Since you're out here, maybe you can take my son, Anthony, to school," she says.

I don't want to go to school with him, but Mom explains that he's a policeman and he's here to keep an eye on our house in case my father shows up. She makes fun of him for not being clever enough to stay hidden. That's how I end up riding to school with the policeman. His face is oily and pockmarked. I start calling him Mr. Pizza Face in my head.

I stay quiet on the car ride because Mr. Pizza Face looks mean. The car stinks of cigarettes and old sandwiches, and he listens to a stupid radio show where all anyone talks about is politics and old movies I've never heard of. I hope he doesn't come to pick me up at school this afternoon.

He doesn't. It's Lise who comes. We don't see the policeman, so maybe he listened to our mom and is spying on us from some hiding spot. At dinnertime, Lise and I are allowed to watch TV, which is how we're getting updates on Dad. He was spotted on a country road. A woman says that she was afraid of him but that he didn't harm her; he just wanted her to drive him to—

Mom shuts off the TV without a word. Lise takes me to her room. As I climb the stairs, I turn my head and see my mom with her face in her hands.

That night, I sleep in Lise's room.

We turn off the light and make a tent under the sheet.

"Do you think he'll be able to get away?" I ask.

"I hope not."

"Are you crazy?"

"You're the one who doesn't understand," Lise says. "When you escape and get caught again, you get a longer prison sentence. So the more Dad runs, the longer he'll be in jail."

"But he might not get caught."

"If he doesn't, he'll never live in peace. The police will always be chasing him."

I sigh. "I guess you're right. Do you think Grandpa helped him escape?"

"Maybe. But I can't imagine Grandpa on a scooter. And on TV, they said that's how Dad got away."

"Yaya, then?" I say, even though it's hard (and pretty funny) to picture my grandmother on a scooter. She's afraid when we ride our bicycles.

"You're nuts!"

"Where will Dad go?" I ask. "You think the police are watching everywhere?"

"Probably. But I bet he knows that. It's better not to think about it."

"Can we do hot water bottle?"

I put my feet over Lise's and we fall asleep.

. . .

Lise leaves a few days later. Just takes off.

She says she's going to her friend Aïssata's, but around nine o'clock that evening Mom starts to worry and calls Aïssata's house. Lise isn't there. Then Mom calls Yaya and Grandpa and all three of them go looking for Lise.

For the first time, I'm home alone. I start to get scared. I hear strange noises, and the streetlights cast creepy shadows through the windows. I feel anxious even though I know I'm being silly. I go to Lise's room and play some CDs. Normally I'm not allowed to touch them, but today is different. Then I turn the lights on in every room: my mom's bedroom, the living room, the kitchen, even the bathrooms. I turn the TV on for company. I check behind doors and under furniture to be sure no one is hiding. I feel better, less afraid. I lie down on the couch and see what's on TV. I channel surf but nothing interests me. I watch a DVD instead; it's one I've seen, and it's funny, but this time it doesn't make me laugh. Later I get up and go back to Lise's bedroom, where I notice that she took her diary, along with her favorite CD and her pajamas.

I start checking my watch constantly, but time is moving really slowly.

Through the window, the policeman watching our house signals to his approaching replacement that something is going on. I look at them and they look back at me. At least if the police are here, no alien or monster will leap out of my closet and kidnap me. But monsters are stronger than policemen. I open the window in case some monster does attack me. That way I can shout for help.

The policemen talk to each other and make phone calls. I want to go out and speak to them, but I know it would be a big mistake. But what if they could find my sister?

Much later, my grandparents and mom come home. Lise is with them and no one is scolding her. She has her big backpack with her; I didn't notice she had taken it. They're all very calm, trying to act normal, not like when Yaya talks loudly, Mom yells at Lise, and Grandpa grumbles.

"Anthony, what's all this noise?" Mom asks. "I could hear it from the other end of the street."

I don't want to tell her that I was afraid to be alone.

"I wanted the police to think there were a lot of people home, that's all."

"Really? Well, we're all back now. You can go to bed."

Mom gets a snack for Lise, and Yaya comes up with me to tell me a story. I love my grand-mother's stories—they're better than my mom's and they last longer—but tonight I'm not listening.

"What did Lise do?" I interrupt her.

Grandma frowns. "A stupid thing, that's what Lise did. Don't ask her about it."

Why? Why can't we ever talk about impor-tant things? I wonder.

I've been going to school with Mr. Pizza Face every day since that night. He also picks me up in the afternoon.

After a few days, something happens. It's the day we have a natural science lesson at school and draw animals and plants. Mr. Pizza Face doesn't pick me up in his car; he's on foot instead. We're walking home together and I'm telling him that Hassan and I are friends again, but he isn't listening to me (anyway, it's not true: Hassan is friends with Bruno now—and I hear Bruno's good at jigsaw puzzles). Mr. Pizza Face keeps turning around because there's a man following us and taking pictures. The policeman tells him to stop and get lost, but the guy answers that he's only doing his job and that he's got something called freedom of the press on his side.

When I get home, Mr. Pizza Face goes back inside his smelly car and opens his newspaper. The man who followed us rings the bell. Lise is munching on a candy bar as she opens the door.

"Hi, I work for a newspaper and—"

"My mother isn't here," Lise says quickly. "So leave right now or I'll call the cops."

She tries to push him out but he barges in anyway. Lise looks scared. I'm scared too. But the newspaper man peels off his mustache and takes off his blond hair. . . . It's Dad!

"Is that how you greet your father?" he asks us.

"Dad?"

I can't believe it! Lise stands there open-mouthed while I jump to hug him. He tells us how he's been watching us these last few days, even with the police everywhere.

"Are you staying tonight?" I ask.

He shakes his head. "No. It would look suspicious. I'll take a few pictures. I have a letter for your mom. Will you give it to her, Lise?"

Lise takes the letter but doesn't say a word.

"Where are you hiding?" I ask.

"I can't tell you, Anthony."

I want to cry. Why won't anyone tell me anything, ever?

Dad sees I'm upset. "I'd like to, but I really can't. I'll come to see you again soon, I promise."

"And what if I go with you?"

"What about school?"

"I don't want to go to school anymore. I don't have any friends left. Besides, in one week we'll be on vacation."

Dad doesn't want to hear any more about it.

He stays long enough to watch a cartoon with me and Lise. But he leaves before Mom comes home.

When we tell her that Dad came by, she doesn't believe us. Says we're making it up.

"This isn't funny," she says. "Do you think it's easy for me? At work, I'm bombarded with questions and newsmen harass me, and on top of it *you*—"

Lise takes Dad's letter and hands it to her. "But, Mom, it's true."

Mom drops onto a chair and begins to laugh, but not a regular laugh.

"He's mad, completely mad. Was the policeman outside?"

"Yeah, but Dad disguised himself," I say. "He wore a wig and a mustache and pretended to be a journalist."

"Is this true, Lise?"

Lise nods. "Yes, it's true."

Mom starts to laugh again. I can tell she's relieved and proud too. She reads Dad's letter while Lise and I watch the news on TV. They're saying that no one knows the whereabouts of Rafael Cantes. The police are wondering if he went to Italy, where he has friends, or Belgium, or maybe Ireland. Lise and I look at each other. We know he isn't in any of those countries. He was right here in our house—and it's our secret.

Lying in bed that night, I think about Lise and her backpack, and about Dad's visit. What if Lise tried to join him that night she ran away? I want to ask her if she did, but Mom made me promise not to talk to her about it. For once, I know better than to ask.

I'll ask her when we're older.

Now I've decided that *I* want to go away with my dad. And I won't fail.

The next time he comes to visit us, I'll leave

with him. I've already packed my small back-pack, which I've hidden under my bed. I took a flashlight, a thick sweater, my Windbreaker, some sugar cubes for snacks, and my Swiss army knife. I even stole some money from Lise (a twenty-dollar bill).

I'm waiting for Dad to come and get me. I want to be with him. We'll write to Mom and Lise. And when I go to school again, it will be someplace far away, under a different name, where no one will ask me nosy questions. Mom and Lise can join us later, and when the four of us are together again, we'll go to the movies, on vacations, and on picnics, and on Sundays I'll do jigsaw puzzles with my dad.

Eventually the police will forget to look for him and he'll get a regular job and pay back the money he stole from the banks, and we'll be able to come back to our house.

Lise and I wonder what disguise Dad will think of next time.

"Mailman."

"Garbage collector."

"No, that's lame. Plus it stinks."

"Policeman?"

"Not bad."

"Hunter."

"Singer."

"Journalist."

"Not twice in a row."

We make a bet: Lise says he'll show up as a cop and I say he'll be a mailman. We have our answer a few days later, on the second day of vacation. Lise is in her room with a friend (they're rehearsing dance choreography for a show at summer camp) when someone rings the bell. It's an old man I don't know. He winks at me.

"Dad?"

He nods. I let him in. He eats while I stare at him, and we talk.

"Lise is upstairs with a friend," I tell him.

He seems disappointed.

"Doesn't matter. I can't stay long. I just came to say hello. Please give this to your mother."

He hands over a package. I put it in the hall

closet for safekeeping; my mom will see it when she comes home. Dad goes up to say hello to Lise (pretending to be a friend of Grandpa's, though I think she recognizes him) and I go to my room and grab my backpack.

When Dad leaves, I follow him. He notices me right away and stops walking. Mr. Pizza Face looks up and gets out of his car. My dad sees him and turns to me.

"Anthony! Go inside the house immediately," he says softly but firmly.

Dad's trying not to make himself obvious to Mr. Pizza Face and he's scolding me in a whisper. I take his hand. Now he has to stay with me or the policeman will definitely know something is up.

I say hello to Mr. Pizza Face and he asks me who the man I'm with is.

"It's my other grandfather," I say.

"I see. Good evening, sir."

My dad lifts his cap in greeting and we keep walking. Once we turn the corner, he stops.

"What's going on, Anthony?" he asks. "Why are you following me?"

"I want to stay with you," I tell him. "I've got everything I need in my bag. And I've got some money. I left a note on my desk for Mom and Lise so that they won't worry about me."

"But you can't stay with me, Anthony. It just isn't possible. I'm on the run." Dad sits on the sidewalk to think for a moment. "It's too dangerous for you."

"If it's dangerous, why did you escape?" I ask. "Why are you on the run?"

"I don't have a choice."

"You could have stayed in jail. Lise says that if you're caught, you'll be in jail even longer and we'll never be together again."

"Lise doesn't know everything." He looks at me for a long time. "Anthony, I can't stand being in jail. I don't want to go back there."

His answer bothers me. It's too easy. When I don't want to go to school, I don't have a choice.

"Why didn't you think of that before? A lot of bank robbers end up in jail."

"Yes, you're right. But I didn't know what jail is like."

"What's it like?"

"It's too difficult to explain. Now I really have to go."

Maybe I'm too young to understand, but I get up and look straight into my dad's eyes.

"If you don't take me with you, I'm going to tell Mr. Pizza Face that you're Rafael Cantes and he'll have to arrest you."

As soon as I say that, I regret it.

"You wouldn't do that, would you?" Dad asks.

"Yes, I would. Take me with you."

He thinks about it as he looks at me. He's angry, I can tell.

"Are you sure you want to do this?" he finally says. "Have you thought it over? You won't see your mom or Lise. You won't be able to call them. You'll have to sleep without your nightlight. We'll be alone and we won't have much fun, Anthony. This is serious business."

I nod. "I'm sure," I say.

Dad puts his hands on my shoulders. "Okay, come along, then, but only for a little while.

When I really leave, it will be a long time before we see each other again. You'll go back to Mom and Lise. You promise you won't be sad?"

"Promise."

He's wrong if he thinks I'll let him go away again.

• 5 •

The Journey

We walk to the train station. On the way, Dad explains that if someone asks my last name I have to invent one.

"How about Essaouida?"

"Whose name is that?"

"Hassan's. He's my best friend. Or my ex–best friend. Now I don't have any friends."

"Not the right name. It doesn't sound French enough. We'll call you Anthony Martel. That sounds good, don't you think?"

I nod. "Yeah, it's good."

Dad explains what we're going to do. On the

train, he's going to change out of his old-man wig into a different one, and he's going to start speaking with a foreign accent. If someone talks to us, I'm supposed to keep quiet.

"Okay. I understand."

"What's your name, again?"

"Anthony Cantes."

"Anthony!"

I already forgot that I'm supposed to lie.

"Anthony Martel," I say.

"That's better."

We arrive at the train station. I hold my dad's hand tight; there aren't any metal bars here, but my heart beats even faster than the first time I visited Dad in jail. Dad looks at me and smiles, which makes me feel better. He goes to open a locker and retrieves a big backpack. At the ticket window, I don't recognize his voice. His accent is worse than Yaya's.

"Good-eh morning, miss-eh. I want-eh two one-away tickets to Nantes."

The woman hands him two tickets. He thanks her in a language I don't understand. It's weird.

I feel like bursting out laughing and I'm terrified at the same time.

We board the train. I don't know whether I'm allowed to talk or not, so I don't say a word. The controller checks our tickets soon after we pass Saumur; the Loire River is dry and some people are walking on the riverbed, between the sandbanks.

When we get off the train at Nantes, I see a few policemen with dogs. I think they're here to arrest us. My dad takes my hand and we cross the station. I can't feel my legs, probably because I'm shaking so much it's like I'm floating on air. When we pass the policemen, one of the dogs barks. I jolt backward and the policeman holding the barking dog comes over and apologizes. My father tells him that I'm just scared of dogs, not to worry. He has the same accent as when he bought the tickets.

"Don't be afraid," he tells me softly.

Once we're out of the station, I walk with my head down, looking at my shoes, and I hold my backpack tightly.

· · ·

My dad looks around before he talks to me again. He bends down and looks me straight in the eyes.

"From now on, no more blunders," he tells me. "We can't afford to be spotted."

I don't want him to notice but I start to cry. It's not my fault I'm afraid of dogs. How could I have known this one would bark at me? Dad strokes my hair and I stop crying.

"Never mind this time, but we have to be very careful. We have to be invisible. They're looking for me; everyone is looking for me. We can't turn back now, Anthony, we can't turn back."

"Where are we going?"

"To the seaside. I have a friend who's going to hide us."

"And they don't know him?"

"Yes, they do. That's why we have to be careful. You know, dogs can sense when someone is scared. And if you're scared, they come to you. So don't be afraid, that's all."

Easy to say.

I want to go home. Dad was right; being on

the run isn't fun. But if I tell him that now, we'd have to take the train back and I might have to walk past the dog again.

We take the cable car, a first for me. It's like a bus but on rails, and it glides when it moves.

Dad still holds my hand, so tightly that it hurts, but I don't complain. He's looking around. Some policemen board the cable car. I feel Dad's hand shaking. These policemen aren't like the ones at the train station; they have no dogs, so I'm not afraid. My dad turns to me and starts talking in a language I don't understand.

We get off at the very end of the line.

Then we walk along the river for a long time. I don't like to walk, especially not when we could be on a bicycle or in a car. And this road just has factory buildings on each side. It's ugly, it stinks, and my feet hurt. When you're in a car, the landscape changes faster.

At last, we get on a new road where there are no factories and there's less traffic. My dad walks in front of me and waits for me to catch up all the time. I'm afraid he'll scold me, but every time he turns back, he plays games to help me catch up, telling me jokes, teaching me new songs. It's nice of him, but I don't think I can take another step.

I should have stayed home with Mom.

Finally we stop in front of a house. It's dark out. The streetlights have been lit for a while, and there are fewer cars on the road.

Dad stashes his backpack at the back of the house and tells me to wait there while he forces a window open and hoists himself inside. I stay right where I am. Strange insect noises start to give me the creeps. I'm getting cold too, and wish I weren't so far from my bed and my home.

When Dad comes to get me, I follow him in the dark, feeling the walls of the house as I go. Dust gathers under my fingers. At home, my globe glows in the night when I go to bed (and it's out when I wake up). Here there's no light at all.

I get my flashlight out of my backpack. The house is empty and has probably been that way for a while. There's a hole in the roof. Dad bangs on a large mattress and a cloud of dust rises. He takes a down coverlet from his bag and tells me to undress.

"Should I put my pajamas on?"

"You brought them?"

"Yes."

"Okay, put them on. Did you also bring your toothbrush?"

"No, I forgot it." I put my pajamas on. It's cold in the house. I don't want to lie down in this large bed alone: it feels ice cold, and I'm certain there are creatures lurking in it, maybe even a skeleton.

I tell my dad that the mattress hurts my back and that I'd rather sleep on the floor like him. All I want is to sleep next to him, but I don't want to admit it. He comes to lie down next to me and puts his hand on my back, which warms me up. He starts to tell me a story like the ones Yaya tells me that last a long time. I feel my feet get heavy, then my legs, and I fall asleep.

· · ·

The rain wakes us up. It's raining right next to us because of the hole in the roof. It's very early, the sun just coming up, and the air smells of wet grass and cows.

We get dressed. Usually I don't mind wearing the same T-shirt twice in a row, but this time it would have been nice to change because my shirt feels damp. We stop in the village and Dad buys some muffins, a bottle of orange juice, and some sandwiches for the road. We have a morning picnic and drink the orange juice directly from the bottle. It's all good, except for the rain. And I wish Mom and Lise were with us, like on a family vacation.

It rains all day. We walk along the river. In one of my geography lessons I learned that the Loire is the longest river in France. It begins at Mont Gerbier-de-Jonc. All I can think about is how I'm tired of walking along the Loire.

"Are we there yet?" I ask.

"In a while. You want me to carry you?"

I hesitate. I don't want to seem like a baby.

"No, I just wanted to know."

We stop to watch some fishermen. There are several of them, all wearing thigh-high rubber boots. All waiting in the water without moving. I take advantage of our rest to remove some gravel from my shoes. One of the fishermen takes a sandwich out of his shoulder bag. It would be nice to eat with him and ask him if he's caught a lot of fish, but Dad says we can't risk being noticed, that a man with a child is easily remembered.

We eat on a bench farther away. The rain has made my sandwich all soggy, and it doesn't taste good. Plus I'm thirsty and we have no water left. Dad takes an old road map out and tells me to go watch the fishermen.

I stay at the edge of the river. It takes them a long time to catch a fish. They don't talk, and I wonder what they think about all day, standing with their feet in the water.

I think about my mom: I hope she found the letter on my desk. I hope she didn't cry. Then I think about Lise. She's probably upset that I left with Dad, especially since I'm pretty sure she tried to do the same thing and got caught. I wonder if Hassan stopped by to find out if I was sick. We're not best friends anymore, but even so. . . . He and I were supposed to go to summer camp together, after all.

Will my mom tell him the truth?

I want to call Lise. I know I'm not supposed to, but I want to anyway.

We leave the river and take a small road. There's no traffic, so we walk in the middle.

Dad asks me what I want to be when I grow up.

"A journalist," I say.

"Why?"

"To tell the truth. Journalists lie. One of them said that you killed a bank guard."

"Is that the only reason you want to become a journalist?"

"Yes."

"They're not all liars. Some go to countries that are at war and risk their lives to tell the rest of the world what's going on. You're sure that's what you want to do?"

"Yes."

"It can be dangerous."

"I wanted to be a policeman before, but not anymore. All I know is that I don't want to be a thief."

It starts to rain again and we pull our hoods up. Now all I hear is the swishing of our Windbreakers and the rain falling on the road. Soon we're walking in mud—*squish, squish*—and my new Nikes are all dirty. If Mom were here, she'd clean them.

Suddenly I can smell the ocean.

I'm drenched and I start to sneeze. I forgot to bring tissues. Dad takes a sweater out of his bag and tells me to put it on. It's too big, but it's warm and it smells good, just like my dad. He picks me up in his arms. I hang on to him and rest my head on his shoulder. I know that's what babies do, but I don't care. No one's around to tell.

A car approaches and dad lifts his arm to make it stop.

"Our car broke down," he says. "Could you take us to the nearest service station, please?"

The driver looks at me. I sneeze and he opens the door. Dad sits next to the driver. They talk, but I don't listen to their conversation. The driver puts the heat on and I go to sleep in my dad's big sweater.

When I wake up, I'm in a bed. I hear voices. I listen and recognize my dad. It's dark in the room, but I can see a light coming from under the door. My eyes adjust after a while and I start to make out some of the shapes: a bed, a desk, a chair, and a chest of drawers. On the floor, there are boxes with books, toys, and a little lamp. I look for the light switch and knock the lamp over, but I manage to turn it on.

I open the door and walk along the hallway. At the end of it, I see my dad sitting in front of a fireplace. He's talking with a man I've seen at our house before. Mom closes the door when he comes so we can't hear them, or she pretends that his cigarette smoke bothers us and she takes him outside.

Dad adds a log to the fire. Some plates and a

pan are still on the table and it smells like apple-sauce. I'm starving.

"Ah, Anthony, this is Thierry. Do you remember him?"

"Yes," I say.

Thierry gets up and looks at me. I look at him too, even though his gold earring makes him look like a pirate. He scares me.

"Do you want to eat something?" he asks me.

"Yes, please."

Thierry brings me some food. It's dark outside. I don't know where we are, but I can hear the sea and the wind. It's still raining. Thierry says it will clear up during the night.

I eat and watch the flames in the fireplace. Dad and Thierry go on talking, exchanging news about friends. Dad tells me about the man who gave us a lift. Thierry says that Mom called him and that he told her not to worry.

Dad frowns. "What did you tell her, exactly?"

"I just said that my nephew was coming to visit me. I think she understood."

I don't understand what he means, so I just

look at Thierry's arms. They're covered in tattoos. On one arm he's got a Native American with a colorful feathered headdress. On the other arm there's a dagger with something written over it.

When dad gets up to take a shower, Thierry explains that he got the tattoo of the Native American when he was young, with friends who all got the same one. That makes me think Thierry might not be so bad.

I smile. "I wear the same sneakers as my best friend," I tell him.

He pulls up his sleeve to let me look closely at the other tattoo.

"This one I got when I was in jail."

My eyes go wide. "Why did you go to jail?"

"Little boys don't need to know. Are you tired?"

I go back to the room where I slept. I put my pajamas on, but they're cold. I push up against the radiator, and when I feel warm, I go back to bed. Dad comes in to say good night.

"Are you asleep, Anthony?"

"No."

He sits next to me. "We'll stay with Thierry for a few days. The police don't know I'm here. We're safe. Thierry will help me escape."

"So you're leaving again?"

"Yes. If I don't, they'll find me. When the time comes, Thierry will take you home. Mom knows."

"Where will you go?"

"I'm not sure. But you don't have to worry about it. I'm here for the time being."

"What does Thierry do?"

"He works at an oyster farm. He'll show you."

"Why did he go to jail?"

"That's none of your business. Besides, he's out now."

"Will you sleep with me?"

"Yes."

He lies down on top of the bed and we turn off the light. It's easier to talk in the dark.

"Dad, why did you become a bank robber?"

Dad takes a deep breath. "I don't know any-more. Your grandfather taught me and it seemed easy. I'm not a big brain like your uncle, you know."

"It's Grandpa's fault, then?"

"No, that's not what I'm saying."

"Lise says that if Yaya had been a good mom, you wouldn't have robbed banks."

"Lise isn't always right, Anthony. When you're an adult, you make your own choices. And this is what I decided to do. Your grandmother didn't force me."

"But can't you do anything else? Don't you have a real trade?"

"I do, in fact."

"What is it?"

"Woodworker."

Being a woodworker is good, I think. Not as good as a photographer, but still good. "What're you going to do now?"

"I'm going to catch up with some friends."

"To work or to rob banks?"

"I don't know, Anthony."

"I want you to tell me. If I ask Yaya, she'll just lie to me. I want to know the truth."

Dad sighs. "Listen to me if you're a big boy. I never killed anyone. I took money from banks, not from people. Banks are insured, and—"

"Lise says that if everybody robbed banks, then no one would have a real job anymore."

"But not everybody does what I do. What I do is dangerous."

"What if you get killed?"

"I've never gotten hurt."

"Not yet. But maybe one day . . ."

"No. I promise you."

"You got caught. You could just as well get killed."

"I tell you it won't happen to me. Go to sleep now."

I want to say that if he gave back the money, even in installments, we could have a normal life. But he pulls the itchy blanket up to my neck, which means I have to go to sleep.

Dad is still stretched out next to me on the blanket, fully dressed, with his shoes on. He takes up a lot of space, but I like being snug against him and hearing him breathe. It's a lot better than being alone in the room.

• 6 •

The Policeman's Daughter

It's a beautiful morning. From the window of my room, I can see the ocean and the white waves. My dad is outside, smoking a cigarette as he looks out at the sea.

Thierry is at work, so Dad makes breakfast. Then I get dressed in clothes Thierry set out for me, and I read a stack of comic books.

When I get tired of reading, I explore the house. It's a small one-story with a ladder that goes up to the attic. The house is surrounded by trees, so no one can see it from the road. Behind it is the sea. The house is pretty empty inside—no rugs, no pictures or decorations of any kind.

I'm bored. I wish I could go to summer camp with Hassan, and I miss the fights I have with Lise. I wish my life could be normal.

I ask Dad to give back the bank money so we can live like everybody else, with Mom and Lise. He doesn't answer me, just strokes my hair.

Dad is listening to the radio (there's no TV in the house) when Thierry comes back at lunchtime. Thierry's brought some mussels, which he cooks in white wine. I've never had white wine before—Mom doesn't want me to. Once, Lise and I tried some in secret, just to see what it was like. We spat it out right away; it was too sour. But Thierry cooks the mussels directly in the wine and it tastes good.

By the time Dad and Thierry are drinking their coffee, I'm bored again. I ask them if I can call Lise. They exchange a look. Dad hesitates and I think he's about to give in, but Thierry shakes his head. I ask if I can write to her instead. Thierry gets up to get some stationery.

I start my letter. I don't really know what to say to my sister. I don't want her to be sad that she isn't with us, but I want her to understand that her brother the shrimp managed to leave with Dad even though I'm younger than she is.

Dear Lise,

Being on vacation with Dad is nice but we have to walk a lot. He slept with me last night but it wasn't like sleeping with you. We didn't do hot water bottle and we didn't make a tent under the blanket. I ate mussels cooked in white wine, which was very good. I saw fishermen. We had a picnic for breakfast.

XOXO,
Anthony

I write the address on the envelope and Thierry puts a stamp on it.

I want to go out and play but there's nothing to play with. Thierry closes the kitchen door to speak to Dad. I have nothing to do, so I listen to their conversation.

"A kid is too much of a burden. And if anyone reported him missing . . ."

"Not a chance."

"I'm not saying that his mom alerted the police, but the cops in front of your house must have noticed that Anthony isn't around."

"I didn't have a choice about bringing him. I'll stay here two days, then I'll go. You'll take Anthony back home."

I open the door. "I can go back alone, I'm old enough."

My dad gets up and slaps my face. "Be quiet! Now go to your room and stay there!"

I am so stunned my dad hit me that I don't feel my face burning right away.

When Dad realizes what he's done, he mumbles that he didn't mean to hurt me, that he just lost control. I don't think I said anything wrong. I run off. Dad tries to catch up with me, but I slam the door of my room (just like Lise does with me) and I tell him I don't want to see him.

I hear Thierry say that I'll calm down in a little while.

They turn the radio on. Quietly, I open the door and tiptoe back to listen to them. They don't mention me. My father wonders what my mom told the police so that they don't suspect anything.

I wonder why I was stupid enough to want to follow Dad.

My cheek is still burning. I shouldn't have forced him to take me along. I head back to my room.

A while later Thierry knocks on the door and comes in. I turn my back to him on the bed. I don't want him to see that I was crying.

"You're taking me home?" I ask.

"Not yet. Have you ever gone sailing?"

I sit up. Thierry is looking at me, smiling. He seems nicer now.

"I sailed once on a lake, with Yaya, my grand-mother."

"Sailing on a lake doesn't count. Come on, let's go! We're headed to the bay. You'll have fun."

I don't know if it's going to be fun, but I have no choice but to follow him. I don't dare tell Thierry that I was seasick out on the boat. He's a big guy, so if he slaps my face . . . He takes me to the attic and makes me try on an old wet suit and a pair of rotten Top-Siders. He says that the wet suit was his son's and that I need old shoes because my feet are sure to get wet. I don't want to put them on. They're totally ratty!

Thierry stares at me with his big eyes and I'm afraid he'll scold me, so I put the shoes on. My dad is sleeping. Thierry looks at the ocean and we head off.

Thierry walks barefoot, even over the gravel along the embankment. He's going so fast I have to run to keep up with him. The wind blowing in my face slows me down.

He raises his arm—the one with the dagger tattoo—and points toward a beach dotted with sailboats and motorboats.

When we reach the sailing club, I feel dizzy because of the wind. Thierry points to a girl about my age and tells me to go see her. I'm going to be paired with her since I'm a beginner.

I walk over to her. Her long hair is all tangled in front of her face. She notices me looking at her.

"Hi. Is this your first time?" she asks.

"Yes."

"Are you related to Thierry?"

"Yes."

Thierry's talking to a friend, but he comes over to us and the girl kisses his cheek.

"You'll take good care of my nephew, won't you, Noemi?"

"Sure. I didn't know you had a nephew."

Thierry winks. "You don't know everything about me." He puts his hand on my shoulder. "Anthony, this is Noemi. Noemi, Anthony. Now, have fun, you two." And he heads back to work at the oyster farm.

The girl shows me around the boat. She explains the use of each rope. She shows me how to tie all the different nautical knots, but it's really hard. I'll have to practice a lot.

"Your uncle is a nice guy," Noemi says. "Did you come for the village fair?"

I hadn't heard about any fair, and Thierry

didn't tell me what to say if anyone asked what I'm doing here. Instead of answering Noemi's question, I ask her how we're going to leave the shore. I notice that she's wearing sailing shoes that are just as ugly as mine, with worn-out treads. They make me forget my own decrepit shoes.

We launch the boat. Noemi does everything. I just enjoy the ride. I look out at the water: it's blue, brown, or gray—gray most of the time. I try to pinpoint Thierry's house, but we're leaving shore so fast that the houses quickly become little white dots.

I don't say a word to Noemi because I'm afraid she'll think I'm stupid. We sail for two hours without talking.

When we return, she walks barefoot like Thierry, holding one wet shoe in each hand. The wind is at our backs now, pushing us. We extend our arms in front of us and let the wind propel us forward. We start talking about Noemi's school, her friends. She asks me if I'm a good student. I tell her about Hassan, about level four of a video game where I'm stuck. Then she asks if I have a girlfriend.

"No. Do you have a boyfriend?"

"I did, but not anymore. He kissed my best friend."

I'm relieved. She asks me why I'm here early in the season. Usually tourists arrive around the end of June. I think about saying that I just had an appendectomy and came to rest at Thierry's, but I don't want to lie to her. I just say that I came with my dad.

"Does he work at the oyster farm too?"

"No. He came to see Thierry."

"Is he Thierry's brother or your mother's brother?"

I have to think fast: if Noemi meets my dad, she'll notice that he doesn't look like Thierry.

"He's my mom's brother," I say.

"He's nice, Thierry. Did you know he's been in prison?"

"Yes. But how do you know that?"

"My father told me. He's a policeman."

I stop breathing. Noemi's a nice girl, but when

Dad learns that her father is a cop, I bet he won't let me see her again.

We reach the end of the embankment. To get to Thierry's house I have to keep walking on the sand. Noemi points to a house at the end of a street.

"That's my house. Want to come over for a snack?"

I want to say yes, but I'm afraid to meet her father. What if he's seen my picture?

"I don't think—"

"Come on, no one's home. My mother's out and my dad's at work until tonight."

If her father is away, I guess I can go. I take off my wet shoes and walk barefoot too. The gravel digs into my heels, but it doesn't hurt too much. Anyway, Noemi isn't complaining, and I'm about to have a snack at her house.

We eat thick slices of chocolate cake and watch TV: we like the same cartoons. She explains what happened on episodes I missed. It's one of the best afternoons I can remember, and one of the best cakes I've ever eaten. Then the phone rings.

When Noemi hangs up, she tells me her father said he's on the trail of a bank robber who's been on TV and to tell her mom he'll be home late tonight.

My heart stars beating fast and I feel my face get hot. I look at the clock and say that I have to go.

I behave stupidly. I want to explain about my dad. I want to tell her that today is the first time I've felt normal since my dad's picture was shown on TV. I want to say that sailing was great, that I wish we could be friends, that I'd like to come to her house every day, but I leave in a hurry, almost without saying goodbye.

I run to Thierry's. I don't think about the fact that Dad slapped my face. Just about how he has to flee.

"Dad, they're looking for you!" I shout as I open the door.

He's reading a book. "Who is 'they'?" he asks, putting the book down in a flash.

"The cops! We have to go!"

My dad jumps up. While I tell him about Noemi, sailing, Noemi's dad on the phone, and the cake, Thierry rushes in, out of breath.

"Rafael, they came to question me."

"Anthony just told me. Where do I hide?"

"We'll go during the night. For the time being, stay put. You're okay here until tomorrow. Did the neighbors see you?"

"No. But they saw Anthony."

"That's all right. I told people at work that my nephew is visiting." He turns toward me. "Anthony, remember, if anyone asks you, you're my nephew, got it?"

I nod, shaking. I want Mom. I want to talk and fight with Lise, to play video games with Hassan, to stay silent on the sailboat, and to eat cake at Noemi's. I don't want my dad to go away. I don't want to say that Thierry is my uncle. I don't want the police to question me.

Dad sits me on his knees. "I'm going into hiding, Anthony. Don't tell anyone, not even your new friend, understand?"

"I want to go with you."

"No, not this time."

Thierry is looking at us. I lean close to my father's ear so Thierry won't hear me. "I don't want to stay with him," I whisper.

"He's my friend, Anthony, he's helping me. You're going to sleep here. I won't be far."

"You promise?"

"I swear."

To delay going to bed, I ask Dad to turn on the radio and play cards with me. He sighs and helps me put my pajamas on. He starts to tell me a story—something about an underwater treasure and a prince who becomes an outlaw. I don't remember exactly.

When I wake up, Dad is gone.

I hear noises in the kitchen. Thierry is doing the dishes. As soon as he sees me, he turns off the radio and folds the newspaper.

He makes me a cup of hot chocolate. I take a look at the paper. There's a picture of my dad on the front page, the one that we saw at home on TV, where you can't recognize him.

"Don't worry," Thierry says. "He'll have to leave sooner, that's all."

"Can I see him one last time?"

"Of course. Tomorrow night's the village fair. I'm in charge of the fireworks. Your father will help me set them off and then he'll disappear."

"What if someone recognizes him?"

"That won't happen. It'll be dark. You'll be able to say goodbye then. I'll take you home to your mom afterward."

Thierry holds my hand on the way to the sailing club. He has huge, hairy tarantula-like hands that crush mine. He points to some huts built on stilts, with large nets hanging out. There are many of them, close to each other.

"We call that a fishery," Thierry says. "Your father is there, in the third hut. We'll see him tonight."

Noemi is waiting for me at the club. Her hair is tied up because of the wind. She waves to Thierry. I want to ask her about her father's search but I'm afraid she'll suspect something.

I want to talk to her but I don't know where to start, so we don't speak.

When we're out on the bay, she gives me the tiller. She's looking straight at me, which makes me uncomfortable. I'm not thinking about my dad anymore.

"Do you want to be my boyfriend?" she asks me.

Next thing I know, we've capsized into the water. I don't know what happened. While we hold on to the daggerboard, a monitor comes over on his own sailboat and helps us lift up our sail. I'm so embarrassed! I don't even look at Noemi.

We don't say anything as we head home. She walks in front of me, barefoot, and I follow her in my wet shoes. I want to say I'm sorry about the boat, but I can't utter a single word. I just keep on walking behind her. Finally she turns back and takes my hand. We sit on the embankment.

"Want to kiss me?" she asks.

Of course I want to kiss her

.   .   .

We eat a snack at Noemi's house and she asks me if I want to stay longer; she says we can call Thierry to see if it's all right. I would really like to stay, but I'm worried about her father seeing me. And I'm right to worry. Her dad comes home a few minutes later. He looks me in the eyes and I'm afraid he'll recognize me. But he nods and smiles.

"Your parents won't wonder what's keeping you?" he asks.

"They will," I say. "I'd better go now."

I say goodbye to him and Noemi walks with me to Thierry's. We kiss. She says that it would be nice to sail together tomorrow.

I take a shower. Thierry brings me dry clothes and asks if I want to go see my dad.

"Can I?"

"The police think he left on a boat," Thierry says. "Put a sweater on and we'll go to him."

Dad is waiting for us on the beach, hidden by the rocks and the darkness. He asks me what I've been doing and if I'm not too bored. I don't want to tell him that I have a girlfriend, so I talk about sailing and how the boat capsized. I want to ask him when he's leaving, whether he'll come back soon, and if he'll send me postcards. But he's the one who asks questions first.

"Will you help me with the fireworks?"

"Since when do you know how to make fireworks go off?" I ask him.

"Do you want to help or not? We can fire the last one together."

"Sure."

Thierry goes up to the hut and lifts the nets. Dad grabs some sand in his hands and tosses it away. The wind sends it back in our direction.

"Let's go in," he says.

It's raining lightly, which I didn't notice before. We go in to see Thierry. The hut is very small, with just a stove and a bed. The floor is made of badly joined planks; the wind comes up through them and I can hear the sea under our feet. The floor creaks. On the bed, I see a pair of binoculars.

Dad shows me a small window through which he's seen me walking to the club with Thierry.

With a flashlight, we watch Thierry leaning over his nets. He's caught one big fish and a lot of small ones.

We leave Dad and head back to Thierry's house. On the way, we come across some policemen. Thierry takes my hand and says hello to them.

"Are they looking for my dad?" I whisper when we've passed them.

"Yes. But they won't find him."

"It's all my fault."

"No, Anthony, it's not your fault."

"You're lying. I heard what you told him."

"He shouldn't have brought you with him, that's true. It's dangerous for you and for him. But even without you, they'd be looking for him."

I fall asleep all by myself, with no night-light, and without feeling scared.

· 7 ·

The Pyrotechnician

Thierry wakes me up early, right in the middle of a great morning dream. He opens the shutters; it's gray outside and the rain knocks against the windows. He's not going to the oyster farm today. Instead, he's spending the day in the village to prepare for tonight's fair. He has to set up the trestles and the boards for the dance floor, and he says I have to go with him. I'd like to tell him that I'd rather go sailing with Noemi.

"Can I come this morning and go sailing this afternoon?" I ask.

"Sure, if you like. Sailing is fun, isn't it?"

"Yeah."

I don't tell him that what I especially like is being with Noemi.

In the village, everyone knows Thierry, so I can walk around without any problem. Shopkeepers even give me gifts: a pencil with the name of the village written on it, and a cap. Thierry introduces me to everybody as his nephew.

The supply of fireworks for tonight is stored in a shed near a church. Thierry takes me there and tells me that I'm going to help him carry the load to his truck. I just have to be very careful, since firework shells are fragile.

"And my dad?"

"We'll meet him later on the beach to prepare for tonight."

"What if someone spots him?"

"Not likely. I do the fireworks every year, and somebody always helps me. There's no reason for anyone to think it's your dad. Besides, they believe he's already gone."

Thierry still has more to do after I finish loading the shells into the truck. He tells me to go wait in the church. There's no one in there. Near the altar among the candles, I see a boat all made of gold, real gold. Even the sails are gold. Since I'm alone, I touch it. It's cold and smooth. I've never touched so much gold before. Whenever I've visited castles, which always have a lot of gold, the tour guide always warns everyone to keep their hands off everything.

Thierry honks his horn and I come out of the church.

"It's nice in there, isn't it? Some fishermen had it built to thank God for saving their lives in a storm."

"I don't know if I believe in God."

"Well, I do."

We reach the dunes. Dad comes down from the hut and sits in the back of the truck.

We drive up to the wet sand; then we walk on the beach and Thierry starts to dig holes.

"Just dig holes like mine, Anthony."

"Deep?"

"Like mine."

A fine mist starts coming down. There's no one else on the beach. We dig holes to put the shells in. They have to hold until tonight, so we'll cover them with plastic trash bags and cardboard boxes to protect them from the rain and wind.

Thierry is showing me the shells when I notice a shape farther out. Dad jumps up right away, tense. Thierry squints to try to see who it is.

"It's okay," Thierry says. "It's Noemi, the cop's daughter."

"Go see her, Anthony."

"Can't she come here?"

Thierry and Dad look at each other and Thierry nods.

"I'd like to show her the shells," I say.

"If you want."

I run toward her. She's barefoot, even though it's freezing. I'm happy to see her, because this time I'm dressed in my regular clothes, and wearing my Nikes instead of the rotten Top-Siders Thierry lent me.

"Hi," I say.

"Hi. What are you up to?"

"I'm helping Thierry with the fireworks. You want to see a shell?"

"I thought kids weren't allowed?"

We go together to look at the shells. Noemi asks questions, which Thierry answers, and I help my dad unroll the yellow ribbon that will mark off the security perimeter. Since fireworks are dangerous, Dad says it's important to keep people from coming too close. Thierry begins putting the shells in the holes.

Noemi goes to get sandwiches and juice, and we have a picnic on the beach even though the weather is bad. It's like being on vacation, minus Mom and Lise. Lise always complains that she's tired of picnics.

After we eat, Noemi and I leave Thierry to go to the club. Dad's not around anymore. Thierry signaled me to go and not to worry. I think Noemi saw us exchange a look. Maybe she understood what it was all about.

· · ·

On the water, I see motorboats patrolling between the sailboats.

"It's my dad! There on that boat!" Noemi shouts.

Noemi gestures wildly with her arm, and a Zodiac comes close to us. Her father is wearing his uniform, and he's with other policemen. We ask him what they're doing.

"We're watching for Rafael Cantes. He's in the area, so we're inspecting all boats."

Thierry is wrong. They're still looking for my dad. I have to warn him, but I don't want Noemi to suspect anything. If I tell her the truth, I might get back on land faster, and Dad will have a better chance of escaping.

But what if I tell her about Dad and she doesn't understand? Then what? Or what if I tell her and she ends up betraying her father by helping me? If my dad gets caught, I could see him in the visiting room, but if he escapes, I won't see him for a very long time. And if he gets caught because of me, he won't want to see me ever again.

I should have told Dad *why* he has to give the money back. Lise is right; he'll never be free otherwise.

The sailing monitors order all boats back to the dock in case the situation becomes dangerous.

As we're putting the equipment away, the police boats continue to circle and search the remaining boats out on the bay.

Noemi asks me to meet her in front of the club after the fireworks so we can ride the bumper cars.

It's dark now, and the tide is high.

The sand is wet, and our markers are still visible. Thierry, Dad, and I remove the trash bags and the cardboard boxes covering the shells.

People are arriving from the village. We can hear music from the fair and the squeals of excited kids, and the smell of grilled sausages, beer, and chocolate crepes fills the air. It's almost like Bastille Day, only last year on Bastille Day, Lise and I were at summer camp. It was very cloudy and we never saw the fireworks. I fell asleep. But this year that's not going to happen. This year I'm the one who will help light the fuses.

The fireworks are about to start.

I can see that my dad is nervous. He smokes cigarette after cigarette, and I start to wonder how he's able to light the matches before the wind blows out the flames. Thierry is like a watchdog. He zeroes in on people who come too close and tells them to keep away. He talks to them loudly, with that scary, gruff voice of his.

The first shell is fired; it makes a small blue flame. I try to watch it climb into the sky but it goes too fast. I don't have time to see the shower. I see only the last sparks, which are kind of yellow. It smells good. On the embankment, people start to clap. I see my dad smile. He keeps lighting the fuses, quickly now. People keep clapping; the sea is rising; there's a nice light breeze.

Dad and Thierry spring from shell to shell. They remind me of acrobats.

The shells explode in the sky faster and faster, people applaud louder and louder, and the flares form gray clouds that float and fall down quickly. I can't see the real stars, only the blue, red, pink, green, and yellow colors of the flares. I like the blue ones best—the most beautiful, for sure—but there are very few of them.

Suddenly the clapping stops. The crowd starts to part, as if it's making way for something. I hear a siren. Men start to run in all directions. They shout. I hardly have time to see my dad climb quickly into a small dinghy that I didn't notice until now. He thought of everything, I see.

I don't know what comes over me: I help push the dinghy out. Dad starts the motor and says goodbye to me, quickly, in a whisper, but he takes a long look at me. I look at the flares: the final one still has to be fired, the one he and I were supposed to fire together. I've been watching my dad all night, so I know what to do. I light the fuse. If Yaya were here, she'd faint with fear.

The police are running over to us. Thierry looks at them, motionless. He doesn't try to flee: he's waiting for them.

Once they take Thierry away, I'm alone. I take care of the remaining shells, which doesn't give me time to think about anything else. I concentrate so hard that I could make spoons bend just by looking at them.

I see Noemi's father in uniform. I hide so he can't see me, but he's not paying attention to me anyway. He doesn't even seem to recognize me. I hear him swear and he looks on as my dad goes off in the dinghy. He shouts that he needs a Zodiac.

I start to light the fuses of the shells that are laid out parallel to the water. I have to keep the cops from crossing that line. That's all that counts.

It's dangerous and the police know it. I'm a kid who's brandishing big ignited shells at them. They stay back, not expecting this.

They shout for me to step aside. I look out at the sea. It's dark, and the dinghy has disappeared. Noemi's father takes out a gun and shoots. Now I know he recognized me. But it doesn't matter. Since it's nighttime, the police aim red lasers at their target. The target is my dad, and I'm scared.

I keep lighting the fuses, which make a lot of noise. People start looking up at the sky again. Multicolored fireworks explode. They're a lot prettier than the small red dots the cops make on the waves.

But I don't know if the noise is coming from the fireworks or from the sound of gunfire. Everything is confused. I look up at the sky, not wanting to see if my dad is hurt, and I forget that I'm scared.

Thierry is in handcuffs, leaning against a police car. He asks Noemi's father if he can talk to me. The policeman hesitates but signals for me to approach.

"Everything's fine," Thierry says to reassure me. "He had time to reach the boat that was waiting for him. The cops won't catch him."

"He should have given the money back. I told him to, but—"

Thierry puts his handcuffed hands on my shoulder and squeezes it. It hurts, but it feels good too.

The fireworks are over. It's dark and the stars are gone. Shell casings litter the beach. I was supposed to pick them up with Thierry and Dad, but the police are questioning Thierry, and Dad is gone. He left without me. Suddenly I remember that I totally forgot to meet up with Noemi.

I am on my own and I am not afraid. I can hear the distant noise of the police motorboats. They've turned on their lights to illuminate the ocean, and it looks like lots of moons are shining right over the water. But the police don't see anything.

"Rafael Cantes!" they shout into megaphones. "You won't make it! Give yourself up!"

They don't know my dad. If they think he's going to surrender . . .

. . .

Now I have to wait.

Dad will be back. I know it. I don't know when. I don't know where. But I know he'll come back.

And I'll be waiting for him.

About the Author

Clara Bourreau writes screenplays for television and film in France, where she lives.